P9-CET-684

BILL AND PETE

TO THE RESCUE

WRITTEN AND ILLUSTRATED BY
TOMIE dePAOLA

G. P. PUTNAM'S SONS · NEW YORK

37 ♥ DE PAOLA

For all my friends in and from New Orleans:
Coleen Salley, Kenneth Holditch, George Dureau, Marigny Dupuy,
Susan Larson, Kevin McCaffrey, Berthe Amoss, Jimmy Langham,
Don Toler, my "niece" Genevieve, my "nephews" George and David—
and even though I don't know her (but I love her books)—Anne Rice.

—T DEP, N. H.

 G. P. Putnam's Sons, a division of The Putnam & Grosset Group,
200 Madison Avenue, New York, NY 10016. G. P. Putnam's Sons, Reg. U.S. Pat. & Tm. Off.
Published simultaneously in Canada. Printed in Hong Kong by South China Printing Co. (1988) Ltd.
Designed by Donna Mark. Text set in Simoncini Garamond.
Library of Congress Cataloging-in-Publication Data
dePaola, Tomie. Bill and Pete to the rescue / Tomie dePaola. p. cm.
Summary: Bill the crocodile and his toothbrush, Pete the plover, set out to save Bill's
cousin, who has been captured along with other endangered animals and taken from Egypt
to the Bad Guy's Big Bad Brother's Exotic Animal Farm near New Orleans, Louisiana.
[1. Crocodile—Fiction. 2. Birds—Fiction. 3. Endangered species—Fiction.]
I. Title. PZ7.D439Bt 1998 [E]—dc21 97-18684 CIP AC
ISBN 0-399-23208-7
1 3 5 7 9 10 8 6 4 2
FIRST IMPRESSION

There was a lot of excitement on the banks of the Nile, where William Everett Crocodile (who was called Bill) and his friend, Pete (who was his toothbrush), lived with Bill's mama.

"What in heaven's name is going on?" Mama asked.

"Little Jane Allison Crocodile is missing!" Pete said. Little Jane was Bill's cousin.

“How terrible,” Mama said. “Where can she be?”

“At least she wasn’t taken to Cairo to become a suitcase,” Pete said. “The Bad Guy is still in jail for trying to steal the Sacred Eye of Isis from the museum.”

“But he’s the only one who steals crocodiles!” Bill said.

"No, he's not," said the old crocodile, swimming up with news. "The Bad Guy's Big Bad Brother is here from the United States and he steals crocodiles, too. He took little Jane Allison. I saw her being loaded on the *Cleopatra* in the harbor along with a hippo, an ibis, and a camel."

"Oh, my goodness," Mama said. "Whatever shall we do? It's times like these that I wish your father was here, and not a suitcase."

"C'mon, Bill. Let's see what *we* can do!" Pete said.

"OK, Pete," Bill said. "Let's go!"

"Now, Bill, now, Pete," Mama said. "Be careful."

"We will," they answered.

They found the *Cleopatra* in the harbor.

"Smoke is coming out of the smokestacks, Bill," Pete said. "It's getting ready to leave. We have to get on board *now*."

“Wait,” Bill said. “I have to write a note to Mama.” He finished writing and put the note in a bottle and sent it up the Nile.

Bill and Pete snuck onto the ship and became stowaways.

"You wait here, Bill," Pete said. "I'm going to fly around and see what I can find out."

Pete flew all over the ship. He saw sailors working. He saw waiters serving people in deck chairs. He saw a Rich Lady standing at the railing. And he saw the Bad Guy's Big Bad Brother. Pete flew back to Bill.

"He's here, all right," Pete said. "I heard him say that he is taking a hippo, an ibis, a camel, and a little Nile crocodile to the United States of America."

"Cousin Jane!" Bill said. "We have to save her, Pete."

"We will, Bill, we will," Pete said. "But Cousin Jane and the others are locked up below. We can't do anything until we land."

The next day Pete flew over the deck again. The Bad Guy's Big Bad Brother was talking to the Rich Lady. All of a sudden the Rich Lady's handbag flew off her arm. "My handbag," she screamed. "All my jewels!"

Pete flew down and grabbed the handbag just before it hit the water. He flew back up and held it out to the Rich Lady. She grabbed it—and Pete!

“Oh, you sweet little bird,” she cooed. “You saved a fortune. For your reward I’m going to take you home with me to my big beautiful mansion, where I will take good care of you.”

Before he knew it, Pete was hanging in the Rich Lady’s stateroom.

Poor Bill. He waited and waited for Pete. Where could he be? Thank goodness there was a big bunch of bananas nearby.

Days and days went by. No Pete. Poor Bill.
And poor Pete. Day after day, swinging in the cage.

"H-O-O-O-T, H-O-O-O-T," went the ship's horn. The *Cleopatra* had left the ocean and was sailing up the Mississippi. It docked at a big city.

A big door opened. Bill crept up and looked out. He saw cages being put on the back of a big truck. Cousin Jane was in one of them.

Then Bill saw Pete in a birdcage being carried by the Rich Lady. She got into a big car and drove off.

I'd better try and save Cousin Jane first. Then I'll find Pete and save him, too! Bill thought.

As soon as it was dark, Bill crept off the ship and headed up the big river in the direction the truck had gone. He left the big river and swam and swam and swam. Finally he came to a swamp.

"Hey there, what ya doin'?" a voice said. "And what kinda 'Gator are you?"

"I'm William Everett Crocodile, but everyone calls me Bill. I've come all the way from the Nile on a big ship to save my Cousin Jane. She was kidnapped by the Bad Guy's Big Bad Brother."

"Well, how de doo. I am Antoine Pierre Alligator, and you are in the Decatur Bayou in the great state of Louisiana in the United States of America. A whole bunch of us 'Gators live here, so you just come with me, Cousin, and we'll see what we can do to help. By the way, you can call me Bubba."

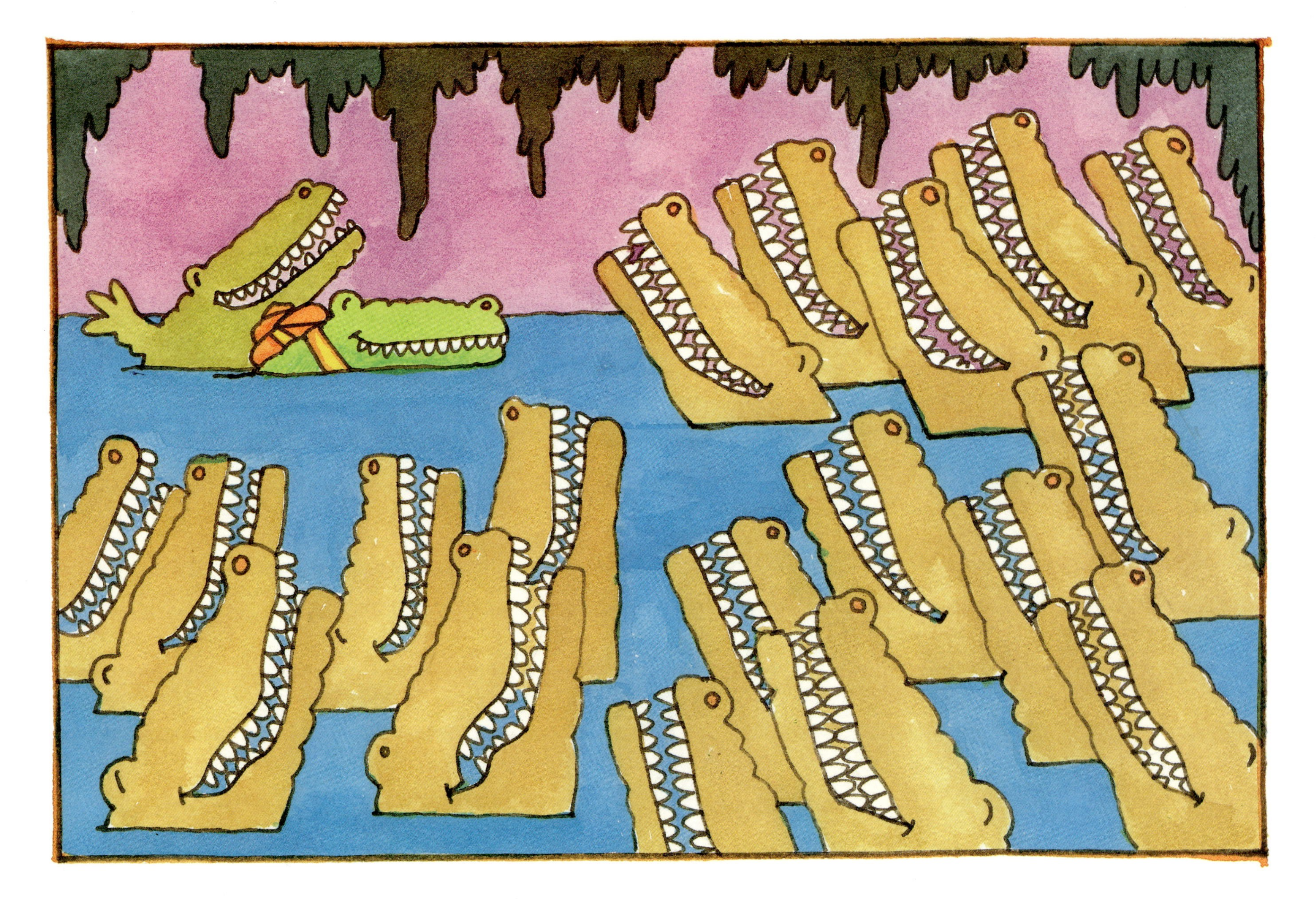

So Bill and Bubba swam deeper into the Decatur Bayou to meet with all the other 'Gators.

Meanwhile in a big mansion in the Garden District of the city, the Rich Lady carried Pete up the stairs to a lovely room at the top of the house.

"Up here at the top, birdie, you'll be able to look out and see the city."

She put Pete in a fancy birdcage. She made sure he had fancy bird seed. She even brought a radio so that Pete would have company when she was out.

A big moon filled the night sky. Pete looked out over the lights of the city. A tear rolled down his cheek.

"It is lonely up here at the top," he said to himself.

Under the same moon, Bill and his 'Gator cousins came up with a plan. One 'Gator knew where the Bad Guy's Big Bad Brother's Exotic Animal Farm was. They would go there and free the animals.

Pete was so sad. He gazed out the window, listening to music on the radio.

"We interrupt this program to bring you this news flash. A large group of alligators is coming over the levee in the French Quarter. One of the 'Gators is bright green, not like any 'Gator seen in these parts before."

"Bill!" shouted Pete.

Just then a maid came in. “Here I come, birdie, to clean up your cage. But first, let’s open the window and let some fresh air in here.”

And let me out, thought Pete.

Sure enough, as soon as the maid opened the cage, Pete flew out.
Free at last. Now to find Bill.

There was Bill at the head of a line of alligators heading toward the B.G.B.B.B. Exotic Animal Farm, followed by reporters and photographers.

"Bill, Bill," Pete shouted, flying down to his friend.

"Oh, Pete, I'm so glad to see you," Bill said. "Bubba, this is my best friend, Pete, I told you about."

"Happy to make your acquaintance," Bubba said. "Now, let's go get 'em!"

Bill and Pete and the alligators stormed the gates. The Bad Guy's Big Bad Brother's helpers all ran away when they saw the alligators. And there in the cages were the Exotic Animals.

"Why, this is against the law," shouted a reporter. "These are endangered species." And they grabbed the Bad Guy's Big Bad Brother and held him until the police came to take him away.

"C'mon, Pete," Bill said. "We've got to find Cousin Jane." They looked around the cages. They saw a sign: NILE CROCODILE—VERY RARE.

"Cousin Jane, Cousin Jane," Bill shouted. "We've come to rescue you!"
"Oh, Cousin Bill," said little Jane Allison.

A big crocodile crawled over next to little Jane.

"So this is the cousin you've been telling me about," he said. "How brave to come all the way from the Nile to save your little cousin. I used to live on the banks of the Nile," he told Bill. "Have you lived there all your life?"

"Yes, sir," Bill said. "This is Pete, my toothbrush—and my best friend. My full name is William Everett."

"William Everett," the big crocodile said. "Do you live with your mother and father?" he asked.

"Just my mama, sir," Bill said. "My father was captured by the Bad Guy of Cairo. He's a suitcase now."

"*No, he isn't!*" the big crocodile shouted. "William Everett, I am your papa! Before you were even hatched, your mama and I decided on your name. Then the Bad Guy caught me and sold me to his Big Bad Brother. I have been here all this time."

"Papa!" Bill said.
"William Everett!" Papa said.

“What a scene, ladies and gentlemen,” a reporter said. “All these exotic animals held captive for years are now free. But what is going to happen to them now? How will they get back to where they belong? Stay tuned and we will bring you a news update as the story unfolds.”

Bubba spoke up. “Bill, you, your papa, your cousin, and Pete, of course, can stay in the Bayou with us.”

“Oh, thank you, Bubba. But Mama will miss me,” Bill said sadly.

“We promised we’d be back,” Pete said.

“Who’s in charge here?” a booming voice said. It was the Rich Lady. She had heard everything on the radio and rushed right over.

“I am sending all of these animals back to their homes. First class. You too, birdie,” she said, looking at Pete.

"Good-bye, cousins, good-bye," Bill and Pete shouted. Papa and little Jane waved.

"Y'all come back now, ya hear!" shouted Bubba.

What a homecoming! Flags flying, bands playing, confetti in the air.

There was Mama, waiting on the dock.
"Oh, Bill, oh, Pete, what heroes you are!" she said.
"Look who's with us, Mama," Bill said.
"Papa! My dear husband! How I have missed you!"
Papa hugged Mama.

"Now we can all live happily ever after as one big family," Papa said, "because Bill and Pete came to the rescue."